Sharing With Our Neighbors

by David Parker
Illustrated by Margeaux Lucas

Scholastic Inc.
New York   Toronto   London   Auckland   Sydney
Mexico City   New Delhi   Hong Kong   Buenos Aires

To Mrs. Moore.
— D.P.

For my beloved Grandma Lucas.
— M.L.

ISBN-13: 978-0-439-87128-0
ISBN-10: 0-439-87128-X

Text copyright © 2007 by David Parker
Illustrations copyright © 2007 by Margeaux Lucas
All rights reserved. Published by Scholastic Inc.
SCHOLASTIC and associated logos are trademarks and/or registered trademarks of Scholastic Inc.

12 11 10 9 8 7 6 5 4 3 2 1   7 8 9 10 11 12/0

Printed in the U.S.A.
First printing, March 2007

Chapter One
Priority Mail

My class writes letters to our pen pals at the senior center every week.

My pen pal's name is Millie Jackson.
But I call her Miss Millie.
She has two daughters, one son, and
five grandsons.
Miss Millie says she always wanted a
granddaughter, too.

I am six. Miss Millie is eighty-six.
We are almost alike.
I know because she sent me pictures.
Her name is Millie. Mine is Jilly.
We both have brown hair and
red shoes.

I write to Miss Millie about my first
ballet show.
I tell her that my dog Fred can sit
and stay.
I wish my brother would stop pulling
my braids.

Miss Millie tells me about her trip
to Florida.
Her parrot, Petunia, says, "Millie is
silly. Silly Millie."
She wishes the senior center would
serve brownies instead of rice
pudding.

Today is Mail Day!
We get invitations instead of letters.

You're Invited To A Party!

Who: Mrs. Hall's class

What: Games, desserts, and more

When: Friday, 1 p.m.

Why: Spend the afternoon with your pen pal!

"What a nice surprise!" Mrs. Hall says.
"Can we go?" Brandon asks.
"Of course," says Mrs. Hall.
Everyone cheers.

Chapter Two
Express Delivery

"Let's make cards for our pen pals,"
says Simon.
"We can deliver them ourselves,"
says Amanda.

My card is extra special.
It has a picture of Petunia on the front.
I glue real feathers to it.

"Your pen pals are sharing their home with us," Mrs. Hall says. "What can we share with them?"
"I will tell a funny story," says José.
"I can sing my favorite song," says Grace.

I will bring brownies to the party.
Miss Millie will like that.

At home, I ask Mom to help me in the kitchen.
I get the eggs and butter.
Mom gets the sugar and brownie mix.

We mix and stir the batter.
Mom lets me lick the spoon.
Then Mom puts the pan in the oven.

Ding! The brownies are done.
They smell great!
Mom cuts the brownies into squares.
She lets me save one for dessert
tonight.

I wrap the brownies in pink plastic.
I tie a ribbon around each one.
Pink is Miss Millie's favorite color.

Chapter Three
Sincerely Yours

It's Friday. Time for our field trip!
The senior center has a big, grassy
lawn and a pool in back.
"Welcome," says Mrs. Whitney.
"We're so happy you're here."

"Thank you for inviting us," says Simon.
"We made cards for you," says Amanda.

"I have a funny story to tell," says José.
"I will sing my favorite song," says
Grace.
"I made brownies," I say.
Miss Millie smiles at me.

"You are a very special girl," says
Miss Millie. "I'm so glad you are my
pen pal."

Miss Millie lets me talk to Petunia.
"I taught her to say something new,"
says Miss Millie.
"Jilly is silly. Silly Jilly," says Petunia.

We all play a board game.
Miss Millie and I come in second
place.
We make a great team.

"This was a wonderful visit," says Miss Millie.
"I had a good time, too," I say.
"It's time to say goodbye to our pen pals," says Mrs. Hall.
We will write to each other soon.

Sharing with our neighbors feels good.

What can you do to make someone else feel good?